Tori Tortoise Turns 100

Join Tori on her journey through Arizona,
from a hatchling, to celebrating her birthday,
with the State of Arizona,
100 years later.

Department of the Interior
Bureau of Land Management Arizona

Written by Heather Lausten
Illustrated by Rachel Ivanyi

ISBN - 13: 978-0-9791310-3-5
ISBN - 10: 0-9791319-3-0

Published 2012 by the Bureau of Land Management

www.blm.gov/az
www.blm.gov/education

BLM/AZ/GI-12/001

Tori Tortoise's family and friends had arrived, excited and eager to celebrate her 100th birthday. The desert just outside the bustling city of Phoenix, Arizona, rang with the laughter of her great-grandchildren riding quads along the trail. Tori was having a fabulous time at her party when suddenly she heard a loud crash. Her great-grandson, Tyler, stumbled across the trail where his quad sat upside-down. He had crashed right into a sign that read, "Stay on the Trail."

Tori called to her great-grandson, "Tyler! What are you doing? Why didn't you stay on the trail?"

"I didn't mean to hit the sign. It's nothing but an old desert anyway. I don't know why I have to stay on a trail," Tyler replied as he sat with a sigh on a small rock beside his great-grandmother.

Tori shook her head as she gazed down at Tyler. "Let me tell you a story and maybe then you will understand why."

Several other animals gathered around as Tori began her tale.

I hatched on February 14, 1912, in a burrow beside a giant ironwood tree. The bright sun sparkled against the rocky desert. Spiky cholla cactus, shady mesquite and green-barked palo verde trees surrounded me. In the distance, I could see a desert bighorn sheep meandering toward the rugged Silver Bell Mountains and a cactus wren flying through the sky.

The air echoed with the sounds of life in what is now called the Ironwood Forest National Monument. It was an exciting day to be born!

My brothers and sisters left to explore the desert, but I hesitated, staying near our burrow for hours after they left. I sat beside the giant ironwood tree and watched the sun move toward the horizon.

"What are you waiting for little one? Go see the world," a whispery voice said.

I looked around and spotted a pink and black Gila monster sitting in the shadows of the tree.

"Excuse me. Did you say something to me?" I asked.

The Gila monster shrugged and looked up at the ironwood tree.

"Don't feel bad, the Gila monster doesn't talk to anyone," the mysterious voice said again.

I swung my head around, looking for the owner of the voice, but couldn't find the source. "Who's there?" I asked.

"Up here," it said, and I looked up into the tree but there was no one there. "I am the ironwood tree," it said and rustled its branches at me.

"Trees can't talk," I answered. At least I was pretty sure they didn't talk.

"How old are you?" it asked.

"I am one day old," I replied proudly.

"Well I am over 500 years old, and so I say I can talk," it responded. I couldn't find a reason not to believe it as I was hearing it talk and it was a tree. The tree continued, "It is a very important day, you know. Today they make Arizona a state."

I didn't quite know what a state was, but the ironwood tree seemed to think that was a very important thing. It sighed, "I wish I had the chance to see all the wonderful places in Arizona."

The ironwood tree told me how the wind blew through to tell it stories about all the exciting places that existed beyond the little burrow. Then, the tree made me promise to visit all of Arizona's treasured landscapes that it could not. Before I knew it, I packed my bags and began a journey I would never forget.

3

It took me ten years before I arrived at Bonita Creek in the Gila Box. Giant cottonwood, sycamore, and willow trees lined the creek. I took a break from my long travels in their shade. The quiet trickle of water lapping against the creek cobbles lulled me to sleep.

The sound of chomping and chewing woke me from my much needed nap. When I opened my eyes, I came face to face with a water-logged beaver doing his best to take down my shade tree. He apologized for waking me and introduced himself as Walter.

"I hope you don't mind," Walter said. "I am almost finished with my house and need this tree to finish the roof."

The tree fell to the ground with a loud crash. I scrambled to my feet and helped him drag the heavy log over to his home. He sat with a huff beside the creek to take a break from his work. As we sat together discussing the weather, he fiddled with several sticks, intertwining them into miniature cabins. In the distance, I saw a much larger cabin surrounded by fields and fields of green vegetables. Several mules wandered along a trail leading away from the fields.

"Where are they going?" I asked.

Walter told me about the towns of Clifton and Morenci, where the people mined the mountains for copper. This valuable metal was then sent to factories where it was turned into wires and pipes that brought electricity and hot water to buildings throughout the United States. They grew vegetables and fruit beside Bonita Creek, harvested them, and then sent them up the trail to feed the men hard at work in the mines.

I helped Walter finish building his house of fallen branches in the cool waters of the creek. I would have loved to see the inside, but the only way in was through an underwater entrance. Unlike our watery cousins, the turtle, a tortoise can't swim. So, I said goodbye to my friend and headed off to see where my journey would take me.

Copper Mine

Safford-Morenci Trail

Bonita Creek

Gila River

Thirsty and tired, I arrived at the San Pedro River. I was now twenty years old. Tortoises have lived in the desert for a really long time and don't need much water to survive, but the cool water refreshed me after such a long walk.

Flowers covered the land with bright colors. My nose twitched with the scent of cardinal and monkey flowers. I heard a buzzing in my ear and looked up into the sky.

"Hello, my name is Clara," a black-chinned hummingbird chirped. "Would you like to play with us?"

Suddenly a flock of twenty birds twittered beside me. Their colors blended in with the bright flowers and leafy trees. We spent the rest of the day playing hide-and-seek in the cottonwoods and willows beside the blue-green water of the San Pedro River.

As the day cooled, we watched as people and animals came to the river for the life-giving water that is so important in the desert. I heard a splash and watched as a few children from the nearby town of Fairbank laughed and played in the cool waters.

"Everyone seems so happy here," I said.

"The river makes us happy," Clara responded. "The people love the waters here. Without the river, the animals could not survive and the people could not grow their food. Many towns and cities develop beside rivers just like the San Pedro. This is why the rivers of the desert are so important."

After years exploring the southern lands of Arizona, I decided to head north. I happened across an ancient trail. The clop-clop sound of hooves on gravelly desert alerted me to a burro, trotting up from behind me. His shaggy mane shook as he tossed his head. "Hola tortuguita. Como estas?"

"Oh, I don't speak Spanish," I replied.

"That's alright, little tortoise, I speak English," he answered. "What are you doing out here all by yourself?"

"I am exploring Arizona."

"Then you are in the right place," he brayed. "This is an important historic trail. It has been used by people for thousands of years. It has had many names, but we like to remember it as the Anza Trail."

He introduced himself as Fernando and offered me a ride on his tall back. For days we traveled the trail while he told me tales of the people and animals that had used the trail.

"My ancestors traveled this trail with Captain Juan Bautista de Anza and a group of Spanish settlers in 1776. They passed through here on their way to northern California to establish a new home."

Fernando told me how the people and their horses, burros and mules would camp along the trail. You can still see their influence in the Spanish names, buildings and culture throughout Arizona.

Fernando and I settled down for our last night together. The starry sky flickered like firecracker sparklers. You could see the constellations, Milky Way Galaxy and many of the planets like Mars and Venus. During the super-quiet night, I heard the cries of coyotes and the buzz of cicadas.

The next day, Fernando continued his journey to California, and I went north toward the Salt River Valley.

(scene from 1776)

I wandered through the desert until I reached lands that are now the Sonoran Desert National Monument. Giant saguaros with juicy fruit at the top of their spiny arms towered above me. It was the strangest forest I had ever been in.

The sound of several rattles shaking drew my curiosity. Above, in a saguaro that like looked a giant baby holding its arms out to its mother, were six slithering rattlesnakes.

"Greetings," one of them hissed, "we are the six snake sisters, Sissy, Sally, Samantha, Sandra, Sarah, and Salina."

I gaped in awe as they slithered up the giant saguaro to reach the bright red cactus fruit. When they came back to the ground the sisters shared their yummy treat with me. The tangy juice dribbled down our chins, and we giggled with delight.

In the distance, I saw several families of people walking through the desert with long sticks, laughing and smiling beneath the saguaros. "What are they doing? " I asked.

"They are the Tohono O'odham. They have lived in the desert for a very long time; and every year, they come here to harvest the saguaro fruit just like we did," Sally said.

A woman reached up with the long stick and knocked fruit from the tall cactus arms. Children scurried around and helped to pick up the fruit, careful to not hurt themselves on the prickly spines.

"They will take the fruit home and cook it to make it into a super-sweet syrup," Salina said.

"But I like to eat it just like this!" said Tori with a slurp. "Yum!"

I left the Sonoran Desert National Monument and walked north for days, not paying attention to the path.

"Watch out!" someone cried just as I tripped. Instead of hitting the hard ground like I expected, I tumbled down forty feet into a deep dark mine shaft. Tiny claws grabbed at my shell and halted my terrifying fall, then gently helped me to the bottom where a family of fuzzy ringtail cats created a cushion out of their tails to soften my landing.

"That could have been very bad if we hadn't been here to help you!" a voice squeaked. I looked up into the beady eyes of two California leaf-nosed bats. "My name's Bella and this is my sister Noche."

"We bats like to live in dark places like this, but we come out at night to eat insects and stretch our wings," Noche chimed in.

It was fortunate that my new bat friends were there to save me from the fall.

Gold glittered on their fur and I grew curious about their home and asked, "What is this place?"

"This is the Vulture Gold Mine," said Noche. "People discovered gold in 1863, and it was the richest gold mine in Arizona. Mining has been very important for our state. The gold is used to make jewelry, coins and other useful things for people."

When it was time for me to go, Bella, Noche and some of the other bats in the mine grabbed my shell and lifted me back to the surface. Once I was safe, I noticed a warning sign that read, "Stay Out, Stay Alive!"

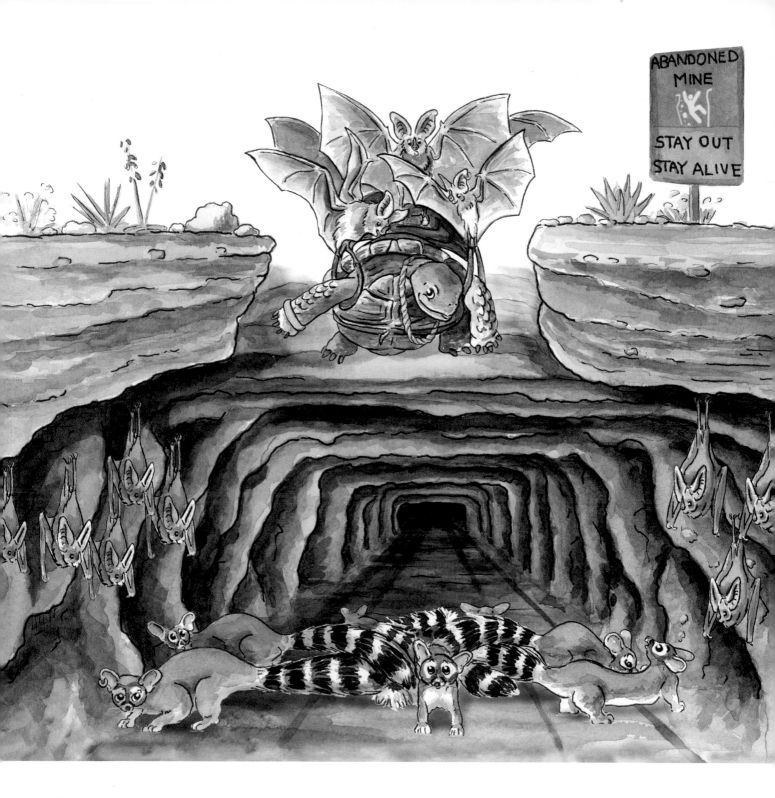

I was very lucky that I didn't get hurt. From that point on, I paid close attention to where I was going. Old mine shafts are dangerous, and I had so many more places I wanted to see. Noche and Bella squeaked a quick goodbye as they fluttered back into the mine. They needed some rest before the evening when they would fly through the sky to find dinner. I waved as I headed down the trail, eager to see where I would find my next adventure.

My journey continued northeast. By this time, I was 50 years old and feeling confident. I learned to watch where I was going, drink enough water, and pace myself in the desert heat. Exploring is tough work after all.

I hiked through the desert, keeping on the trails where it's easier to hike and doesn't harm the rest of the land. I had fallen in love with Arizona and wanted to do my part to keep it beautiful.

Suddenly, I felt a deep rumble on the ground. Turning on my heels, I spied a flock of woolly animals barreling toward me.

"Baaa, excuse me," one called as he passed. Soon they surrounded me, and I felt like a piece of sand inside a cotton ball.

"Who are you?" I asked the last of the animals as they passed me.

"We are sheep. Our shepherds are Basque and have run sheep through the area for generations. They are taking us to have our coats sheared. I am sorry we cannot stay to talk, but we are in a hurry and must go!" and they disappeared down the trail.

I followed them, but the sheep quickly faded into the distance. The trail continued up into the rugged Bradshaw Mountains that were covered in cactus. I took a deep breath and made my way up the steep terrain.

Halfway up the hill, I turned around and gazed out across the land. I could see for miles and miles. Such an awe inspiring sight made all the hard work to get there worth it!

Determined to discover what I could see from the very top, I continued my hike upward. I stepped on loose gravel and lost my footing. My feet slipped out from beneath me and I slid downward. Before I fell too far, my shell hit something and, I came to a stop.

"Hello little tortoise," someone whinnied. I looked up into giant brown eyes. A horse grinned down at me.

"Thank you for helping. That was close!" I replied. I could have rolled all the way to the bottom if he hadn't been there to help.

"My name is Samson. Would you like to walk with me?" the horse asked. "It is safer to hike with a partner."

I agreed, and we spent a wonderful couple of days exploring the Black Canyon National Recreation Trail. I discovered that the trail started out as a route to drive sheep and livestock. In 1969, it turned into a recreation area where people hike, mountain bike, and ride horses, like Samson. We passed a number of people who watched us with strange looks on their faces. I don't think they were used to seeing a horse and tortoise hiking together. But we had a lot of fun, and Samson is still one of my favorite hiking buddies.

A few days later, Samson and I parted ways. I slid down a big canyon to reach a lush green valley and see the great Agua Fria River. Sitting beside a mesquite tree, I listened to the wind and watched the leaves rustle.

"Kuk-kuk-kuk."

I looked around and saw a Yellow-billed Cuckoo grinning down at me from the branches above. "Hello!" she said. "You look like you have been on a long spiral."

"A long *spiral*?" I asked.

"Yes, a long journey. The ancient people that lived here used to draw spirals on boulders to explain their journey." She introduced herself as Miss MacIntyre and joined me in the shade.

"The ancient people would tell their stories by drawing pictures on boulders and cliff faces. Those pictures are called petroglyphs."

Miss MacIntyre took me to see some of the petroglyphs nearby. Pecked into the boulders were images of animals, people and geometric shapes, including a spiral. We also saw the remains of their ancient homes, several pieces of broken pottery, and some arrowheads. "The things these people left behind tell us much about how they used to live. It is important to protect these things, which are called artifacts, by looking and not touching them so that they can be here for everyone."

"You know an awful lot about these ancient people," I said.

Miss MacIntyre twittered at me and ruffled her feathers. "Well I should, I am a teacher and I care very much about teaching others about this place."

She pointed across the river, "I live in a tree beside the ruins of an old 1891 school house. The children that used to go there have grown old, but now I teach the young animals that live here."

"I would love to learn more about the ancient people that lived in Arizona," I told her.

"My friend is taking a trip and will be passing over some amazing sites," she said. "I am sure he would be happy to give you a ride."

I had such a wonderful time learning from Miss MacIntyre and was excited to see what else I would learn on my travels.

Miss MacIntyre's friend Roger was a huge golden eagle. He grabbed me in his sharp talons and beat his giant wings until we soared high above the Arizona desert. Roger didn't say much until we passed the small town of Quartzite.

"Keep your eyes open, little tortoise."

I strained my neck a little to see if I could spot whatever he wanted me to see. We flew several more miles and then I saw a giant image of a man with a spear beside a river full of fish.

"Amazing!" I shouted.

"That is the Fisherman Intaglio. The ancient people scraped the rocks and dirt away to create the images in the ground. According to some Native people, the fisherman represents their creator who carved out the Colorado River with his spear."

Roger wanted to stop to visit some friends at Lake Havasu before continuing our journey so he dropped me off on the rocky shore of the lake and promised to pick me up in the morning.

The water seemed to go on forever into the horizon. Deep blue against the brown hills surrounding it, the lake buzzed with activity. Giant houseboats floated past and smaller speed boats zipped along, creating white tipped waves in their wake. Along the sides of the lake, several smaller boats bobbed in the shallows with fishermen casting lines into the water.

I took a ride on a jet ski and explored the shoreline. Intense sunlight beat down on the lake. There was no shade to be found on the water, so I slathered my skin with sun block and popped on a pair of sunglasses. Even though I was on a lake, I still had to bring plenty of water along for the ride. It is very easy to get dehydrated in the sun; I didn't want to get sick, so I made sure to drink plenty of water.

I put on my life jacket to protect me in case of an accident and then traveled along the waves until I reached a section of the lake that had less boat traffic. I could hear the birds chirping and the wind rustling through the leaves in the bushes and trees along the bank.

I met up with a gangly clapper rail bird named Slim who was fishing in the rushes along the bank. "I see you have prepared yourself for the sun! Too many visitors forget to take care of themselves when they are having fun. Going home with a sunburn or heat exhaustion could ruin a wonderful vacation." Slim warned.

Slim invited me to join him for dinner and introduced me to his family. We had a lovely dinner and spent the night telling ghost stories by the fire. In the morning I helped Slim and his wife wrangle their kids toward the water for fishing lessons. Soon the air thumped with the sound of heavy wings, and Roger the golden eagle returned to the shore.

"Ready to go?" Roger asked.

I thanked my new friends and waved goodbye as Roger grabbed me and flapped his giant wings to bring us high into the sky. We continued north toward the Mount Nutt Wilderness. Roger explained that a Wilderness area is preserved lands where no vehicles are allowed. They are protected lands that provide a secure home to many animals and plants and are a place where people can find solitude and peace.

To the east, I could see the town of Kingman; to the west, I saw the smaller town of Bullhead City. In the distance, a red glow lit up the horizon and Roger turned sharply to bring us to a landing in a field.

"What is that?" I asked, sniffing the thick smoky scent in the air.

"A fire," he replied, worry in his voice. "I must go, little tortoise. A fire is very dangerous for my family and I have to see that they are well."

Roger pointed a long feather to the Northeast. "Head that way and you should be able to avoid the blaze. I am sorry I could not fly you all the way."

Roger took off in a hurry and soared through the sky in a rush to find his family. Roger and I would meet again later.

A rumble of hooves marked the arrival of a herd of burros running from the fire. "Hurry! Hurry! The fire is coming!" They brayed as they thundered past me. I was a little worried since a fire could burn the landscape faster than I could run.

A few minutes later a bighorn sheep stopped his race through the field and said, "You should hurry little tortoise, the fire is moving fast."

"What happened?" I asked.

"Some campers did not put their campfire out completely and the wind pushed the coals into the brush. Now our homes are burning and the fire will be hard to stop." He looked behind with a worried frown then looked to me again, "If you keep going northeast you should be fine. I have to go and check on the rest of the forest and direct others from harm's way."

I thanked him and trundled along as fast as I could. It was sad to think of all the homes that would be lost and the trees and plants that would burn in the fire. A simple campfire seems like such a little thing, but if we aren't careful it can quickly turn into something dangerous and destructive. Luckily, the flames never reached me; later, I learned that Roger's family had been saved too, and the grass and trees grew back better than ever.

Several years later, I reached the lands north of the Grand Canyon. Pinyon pines and sagebrush grew across the grassy fields like sprinkles on a cupcake. Mountains, buttes and canyons stood in my way more than once, and I had to travel around many of them in long detours. It was on one of these detours that I ran into a mule deer named Buck.

"Where are you going?" I asked him as he loped toward me.

"I am going to see the President," he replied. "It is a very special day because he is turning the Grand Canyon-Parashant into a National Monument. I live here and it makes me very excited."

"What is a National Monument?" I asked him.

"Monuments are special lands in the outdoors that are protected so that all animals and people can enjoy them for generations to come."

Buck invited me to join him and we both hiked down the hill toward an important looking man sitting at a table. A mountain lion, Kaibab squirrel, Steller jay, spotted owl and a king snake had also gathered to observe the important event. As we watched the man sign several papers, Buck explained that the man was the President of the United States.

"The land we live on is unique because it is cared for by the Bureau of Land Management and the National Park Service. It belongs to all the people in the country. The lands are places where people can enjoy and explore the great outdoors by hunting, fishing, hiking and camping. It is home to many animals and some of the most beautiful landscapes in the world," Buck affirmed.

They watched as the President finished signing the papers, and everyone cheered in celebration. It surprised me to learn that so many of the places in Arizona that I had visited were actually public lands called the National Landscape Conservation System managed by the Bureau of Land of Management. These treasured landscapes are kept safe and conserved for all of us to enjoy. It made me happy to know I would not be the only one to explore America's great outdoors. These places would be around for my kids and their kids to enjoy.

After celebrating with Buck, I said goodbye and continued my travels. I had promised the ironwood tree that I would visit as much of Arizona as I could and I still had many more miles left to explore.

Laughter echoed across the land. When I looked up, I saw several young girls in buckskin dresses, covered with bright yellow and red beads walking through the grass with their smiling mothers. Curiosity drew me closer.

One of the girls bent over and plucked stems from a low lying bush with yellow flowers and placed them into baskets.

Flapping wings distracted me from the girls. A giant bird with wings wider than a man is tall landed beside me. Her baby plopped to the ground a few feet away. "Pardon us. We don't mean to interrupt, but my condor baby is a tiny bit airsick."

"How can a bird get airsick?" I asked.

"She is still learning to fly and sometimes it upsets her tummy. I stopped here to get some tea to help her feel better." The condor introduced herself as Regina and explained that the stems picked by the young girls are used to make Indian tea. The plant has been used for generations to soothe upset tummies.

"Do you know why the girls are wearing such colorful dresses?" I asked.

"They are the Kaibab Paiute children. The young girls have just completed their coming-of-age ceremony. Their mothers bring them out here and tell them to run to the rising sun. They run and run until they grow tired. Then they are told to run even more. Once they are done, their mothers give them those beautiful dresses to wear that signify they are now young women, and everyone celebrates."

Regina explained that the girls had brothers who were also going through a coming-of-age ceremony across the Houserock Valley on the plateau. The boys were on their first hunting trip. When they kill a mule deer, they thank it for giving its life for the people who share the land. The mule deer are essential to the survival of the Kaibab Paiute, and they hold them in the highest respect.

When the girls saw us standing in the field, they giggled and waved and ran off to follow their mothers home.

I hopped onto Regina's back and we soared through the sky. Beneath my feet I saw brilliantly colored cliffs.

"Those are the Vermilion Cliffs," Regina said. "I have a nest there where my family feels safe. There was a time when no condors were left in the wild. But because we have been protected, there are many more of us now." Regina smiled as she flew, the wind rustling her feathers and kissing our cheeks.

As I gazed across the land, I remembered all the places I had been. I traveled from cactus covered desert, through lush river valleys, up high mountains, across yellow colored grasslands and finally arrived here at the

towering cliffs. It took nearly one hundred years, but I traveled through Arizona on a journey I would always cherish.

Each adventure taught me valuable lessons about how to stay safe, enjoy the land and leave it for generations to come. All of the friends I made taught me to love our treasured landscape.

"So you see Tyler, it isn't just any old desert," Tori said as she patted him on the arm. "It is our desert. There are many wonderful things to see and you should go outside to explore Arizona's treasured landscapes. You should always care for these special places because they belong to all of us."

Tyler nodded slowly and smiled. "I would like to see everything that you have seen someday great-grandma Tori."

Tori smiled back at her great-grandson, "Then go explore Arizona and all of America's great outdoors and be careful this time."

With that, Tyler jumped up from his seat on the rock and skipped over to where his Quad had been flipped right-side up by a grinning circle of friends, many of whom traveled with Tori on her journey and returned today for Tori's 100th birthday party.

The day ended with laughter and happiness as all the animals celebrated the tales of the tortoise and her treasured Arizona landscapes.

Follow Tori's Path and Journey through Arizona's Treasured Landscapes

Learn more about the National Landscape Conservation System and BLM
Recreation at: www.blm.gov/az
See the left navigation box and click: "What We Do"
Then click on: "National Landscape Conservation System" or "Recreation"

Ironwood Forest National Monument

Taking its name from one of the longest living trees in the Arizona desert, the 129,000-acre Ironwood Forest National Monument is a true Sonoran Desert showcase. It is located just northwest of Tucson, Az.   Phone: (520) 258-7200

**Established:
June 9, 2000
Presidential Proclamation**

Gila Box Riparian National Conservation Area

The 23,000-acre Gila Box Riparian National Conservation Area is truly an oasis in the desert. It has four perennial waterways - the Gila and San Francisco rivers and Bonita and Eagle creeks. It is located 20 miles northeast of Safford, Az.   Phone: (928) 348-4400

**Established:
November 28, 1990
U.S. Congress / PL 101-628**

San Pedro Riparian National Conservation Area

One of the most important desert riparian ecosystems in the United States, this 57,000 acre area is home to 84 species of mammals, 14 species of fish, 41 species of reptiles and amphibians, and 100 species of breeding birds. It is located 6 miles east of Sierra Vista, Az.   Phone: (520) 439-6400

**Established:
November 18, 1988
U.S. Congress / PL 100-696**

Juan Bautista de Anza National Historic Trail

Commemorating the 1776 expedition to recolonize 240 people and 1,000 head of livestock from Tubac, Mexico through Arizona to San Francisco, California, this trail was later used for Butterfield Stage, Mormon Battalion, pioneer travelers, and for the 1849 gold rush. The National Park Service (NPS) administers the trail in collaboration with BLM in Yuma and Phoenix.
                                   Phone: (623) 580-5676

**Established:
August 15, 1990
U.S. Congress / PL 101-365**

Sonoran Desert National Monument

The Sonoran Desert National Monument contains more than 486,400 acres of Sonoran Desert landscape, the most biologically diverse of the North American deserts. It is located 70 miles southwest of Phoenix, Az.
                                   Phone: (623) 580-5500

**Established:
January 17, 2001
Presidential Proclamation**

Vulture Gold Mine

The Vulture Mine began in 1863 when California's gold rush prospector Henry Wickenburg came to Arizona and discovered a quartz deposit containing gold. More than 5000 people followed him and founded the town of Wickenburg, Az. The mine became the most productive gold mine in Arizona history, producing 340,000 ounces of gold and 260,000 ounces of silver.   Phone: (623) 580-5500

Established: 1863

continued on next page

The Black Canyon National Recreation Trail

This 79-mile trail system parallels Interstate 17 from the Sonoran Desert lowlands in Phoenix up to the high grasslands of Prescott Valley. The trail is designated for hiking, mountain biking and equestrian use. Historically, it was used by valley woolgrowers to herd sheep to and from their summer range in the Bradshaw Mountains and the Black Hills.   Phone: (623) 580-5500

Original Designation 1919
Department of the Interior
"Livestock Driveway"

Agua Fria National Monument

Ranked among America's most significant archaeological and prehistoric sites, this 70,900-acre national monument is approximately 40 miles north of central Phoenix, Az.   Phone: (623) 580-5500

Established:
January 11, 2000
Presidential Proclamation

Fisherman Intaglio / Yuma

This geoglyph (earth figure) is located near Yuma, six miles north of Quartzite, Az. According to Native Americans, this image may represent their Creator carving the Colorado River with his spear. Geoglyphs are difficult to date.   Phone: (928) 317-3200

Lake Havasu / Parker Dam

Whether your pleasure is jet-skiing, kayaking, or simply floating down the river, BLM public lands offer a variety of boating and floating opportunities in Arizona. Parker Dam creates Lake Havasu by blocking the Colorado River. There are 88 shoreline camps along the Arizona side of Lake Havasu, nine miles south of Lake Havasu City, Az.   Phone: (928) 505-1200

Constructed 1934-1938
Administered by
Bureau of Reclamation

Mount Nutt Wilderness

The Bureau of Land Management (BLM) in Arizona is responsible for 47 wilderness areas totaling 1.4 million acres. The Mount Nutt Wilderness is located 15 miles west of Kingman and encompasses 27,660-acres, including a portion of the Black Mountains. Nutt Mountain, at 5,216 feet, is home to the desert bighorn sheep.   Phone: (928) 718-3700

Established:
November 28, 1990
U.S. Congress / PL 101-628

Grand Canyon-Parashant National Monument

Located 30 miles southwest of St. George, Utah, the Grand Canyon-Parashant National Monument is jointly managed by the Bureau of Land Management (BLM) and the National Park Service (NPS).   Phone: (435) 688-3200

Established:
January 11, 2000
Presidential Proclamation

Vermilion Cliffs National Monument

This remote, unspoiled 294,000-acre national monument is a geologic treasure of towering cliffs, deep canyons, and spectacular sandstone formations. It is located 30 miles south of Page, Arizona, and 41 miles east of Kanab, Utah.   Phone: (435) 688-3200

Established:
November 9, 2000
Presidential Proclamation